Stories of
Dinosaurs

Russell Punter

Illustrated by
Cynthia Decker

Reading Consultant: Alison Kelly
Roehampton University

Series editor: Lesley Sims

Contents

Throughout this book you'll see the names of lots of different dinosaurs. Find out how to say them on page 48.

Chapter 1

The wrestling Raptor

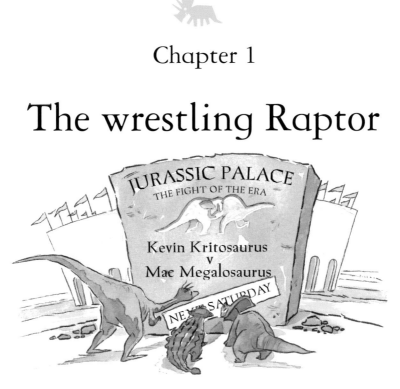

The Dinosaur World Wrestling Final was one week away. Kevin 'Crusher' Kritosaurus was fighting Mac, the masked Megalosaurus.

Kevin's trainer, Reg Raptor, kept him super fit. Every day, he ran fifty laps around the valley...

rowed sixty lengths of the swamp...

worked out in the gym for three hours...

and did five hundred push-ups.

On Sunday, a huge, horned dinosaur lumbered into Reg's gym. It was Stig Ceratosaurus, Mac's trainer.

Hello boys.

"How's training?" sneered Stig. Reg didn't trust his nosy rival. "None of your business," he said.

"Here's some advice, Kev,"
snarled Stig. "Pretend to be
knocked out in the second
round of Saturday's fight."

Hey!

"That way, Mac and I win
the prize money," he added.
"I won't do it," fumed Kevin.
"That's right," snorted Reg.

"Pity," said Stig, as he left. "I only hope you don't have any 'accidents' before the fight."

Kevin and Reg looked worried.

On Monday, Kevin was out on his morning run, when a bridge suddenly collapsed.

Whew. That was close.

Rats.

Splash!

On Tuesday, his rowing boat sprang a leak.

Lucky we can swim.

On Wednesday, a punchbag filled with rocks nearly landed on Kevin's head.

Look out!

On Thursday, someone put red hot chilli powder in his water bottle.

And on Friday, the ropes around the wrestling ring snapped.

PING!

Whooops.

Kevin and Reg guessed Stig was to blame, but they couldn't prove it. It was too late anyway. The day of the big fight had arrived.

"Ladies and gentle-dinos," bellowed the referee, "please welcome today's wrestlers."

Mac and Kevin bounded up the steps to the ring.

Suddenly, Kevin tripped over his tail. He crashed down the steps and landed in a heap.

Woah!

"I can't walk," wailed Kevin. The crowd gasped in shock. Everyone was disappointed that Kevin was out of the fight. Well, almost everyone...

Stig smugly waved a piece of paper at Reg. "The rules say that if he can't fight, Mac and I get the money."

We win, losers!

"We won't let you get away with that," said Reg, enraged.

"But what can we do, Reg?" moaned Kevin. "I can't wrestle."

12

"No, but I can," declared Reg.
Stig cried tears of laughter.
"You? Mac would flatten you in
five seconds."

Ha ha!

"Oh yes?" said Reg, storming
up the steps and into the ring.
The startled referee rang the
bell for the fight to begin.

13

Reg shot across the ring and grabbed Mac by the leg. But no matter how hard he tried, Reg couldn't shift the bulky beast.

Grrr! Ngh!

"Give up, shorty!" yelled Stig. "The prize money's ours." But Reg wasn't beaten yet.

14

He clung on to Mac's tail and
tried to swing him around. The
mighty dinosaur just swatted
Reg like a swamp fly.

Oof!

"Now to finish you off,"
roared Mac. He lunged at the
little Raptor. Reg gulped and
ran for his life.

He darted
across the
ring...

scuttled
between
Mac's legs...

leapt over
his tail...

and ran around
and around
in circles.

Mac was strong, but he wasn't fast. The tiny dinosaur ran circles around him. Mac felt dizzier and dizzier, until...

CRASH!

he thudded to the floor in an exhausted daze.

The referee dangled Reg by the arm in front of the crowd. "The winner!" he declared.

Everyone cheered as Reg and Kevin collected their prize money. And Stig had to drag Mac all the way home.

Chapter 2

Dino diner

Tonight, the Raptor brothers, Mike and Albie, were opening their new restaurant. Mike was writing out fancy menus.

Raptors' Restaurant

"Meet here for meat"

Your hosts: Michael & Albert Raptor

APPETIZERS

Spinosaurus spikes
with a Tarbosaurus dip

Pliosaur platter

STARTERS

Allosaurus soup

Pteranodon Pâté

DISH OF THE DAY

Megalosaurus mixed grill

MAIN COURSES

Baryonyx burger

Cacops chops

Saltopus sausages

Spinosaurus steak

DESSERTS

Pterodactylus pie

Tyrannosaurus tart

Payment: We accept cash
or T-Rex Express Credit Card

Albie polished the knives and forks and ironed the tablecloths. He even folded the napkins into amazing shapes.

Now all that was left was to cook the food. Mike went to the refrigerator. It was empty – no chops, no steaks, not a sausage...

Where's it all gone?

A tiny dinosaur darted through Albie's legs and out the door. A string of sausages dangled from its mouth.

"Come back, you thieving Compsognathus!" yelled Mike. But the rascally reptile was too fast for them.

"We open in an hour," cried Albie. "What are we going to serve to our customers?"

The brothers searched every cupboard and drawer. All they were able to find was a stale Megalosaurus meatball.

"We're ruined," wailed Mike.

"We'll have to cancel the opening," sobbed Albie.

Mike checked the restaurant. "Too late," he gulped. "Our first customer is here."

"Oh no," whispered Albie.
"It's Egon Raptor, from the
Good Grub Guide. If he
doesn't like us, we're done for."

"I need to think," said Mike,
scuttling outside. He always
came up with his best menu
ideas in the fresh air.

Albie kept Egon busy,
pouring him glass after glass
of sparkling swamp water.
Mike spent twenty minutes
pacing up and down outside.

"What use is a restaurant
without food?" he sighed,
sniffing a flower. Suddenly he
had a wild idea.

Mike ran back into the kitchen clutching a huge bundle of plants. "I've got it!" he cried.

"What *are* you doing?" asked his brother.

"I'm going to cook these," replied Mike, excitedly.

"Yuck!" said Albie. "Are you crazy? No one eats leaves."

Mike chopped
up the ferns...

sprinkled them
with moss...

and drizzled it all
with nettle juice.

Hey presto! One
fern feast.

Albie took the dish to Egon's table. He whipped off the silver cover with a flourish. "The chef's special, sir," he announced.

Egon peered at the green pile on his plate. He prodded it with a fork. He stuck his snout into it and sniffed. Finally, he took a great big bite...

"Yeeuch!" he cried, spitting a mouthful across the room. "That's the worst thing I've ever tasted. You'll get zero out of ten in my guide book."

Egon ran out, clutching his tummy. As he left, a strange-looking dinosaur came in.

"Is there any chance of a meal?" he asked politely.

"Not unless you want this," sighed Mike, sliding the plate of leaves across the table.

The dinosaur licked his lips and gobbled it all up. "Very tasty!" he declared.

"You *like* leaves?" said Albie.

"I'm a Stegoceras," replied the customer. "We never eat anything else. Could I have a second helping please?"

The visitor had seven helpings of fern feast. And when he got home, he told all his family and friends about the fantastic food.

From that day on, every meal time was fully booked at the Raptors' new vegetarian restaurant.

Chapter 3

Daisy and the dinosaur

Daisy Dale wasn't enjoying her school trip to the local museum. "Who wants to see a boring old egg exhibition?" she sighed.

On stage stood Professor Hugo Furst, the famous explorer. Next to him were Mr. Bagley, the museum owner, and his wife.

"Good afternoon," boomed the professor. "May I present my latest discovery..."

NATURAL HISTORY MUSEUM

Prof. Hugo Furst's
Egg
Display

GRAND OPENING

TODAY

The professor tugged a sheet to reveal a giant block of ice. Inside was a shiny green egg.

"This is no ordinary egg," he said, proudly. "It was laid sixty million years ago... by a Hadrosaur."

"I discovered it buried in ice at the North Pole," added the professor, waving the sheet around excitedly.

The breeze blew the dust off exhibits nearby... and up Mrs. Bagley's nose.

Atishoo!

Mrs. Bagley bumped
into her husband...

who backed into a
microphone stand...

which tripped up a
museum guard...

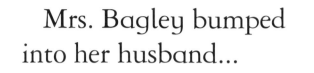

Ouch!

Atishoo!

who fell onto Hugo Furst...

who knocked over the block of ice...

which hit the ground, and smashed into tiny pieces.

Hugo crawled across the floor, searching for his precious find.

"My goodness," said Daisy's teacher. "Let's go somewhere more peaceful and have lunch." She led the class to the cafeteria.

Daisy reached into her bag for her lunchbox. Instead of something hard and firm, she felt something soft and scaly.

A dinosaur!

The creature leaped out in a spray of eggshell. He looked around nervously and ran along the table.

Daisy recognized the broken shell. "It's the Hadrosaur egg," she cried. "It must have landed in my bag and hatched."

As the baby dinosaur raced out, Mrs. Bagley strode in.

Aggh!

Daisy raced after the frightened little creature as he crashed through the museum.

He wrecked the rocks...

smashed the bug bottles...

messed up the meteorites...

and sent the stuffed fish flying.

Daisy couldn't catch him.
Luckily, neither could Mrs.
Bagley. "I want it found and
locked up!" she roared.

Catch it now, professor!

"I can't let them put the
dinosaur in a cage," thought
Daisy. "I must find him first."

"Where would I hide if I were him?" she wondered. "Of course," she cried, rushing to the prehistoric display.

Daisy was right. The baby was snuggled up to a model Hadrosaur.

Honk!

The museum guard appeared,
led by red-faced Mrs. Bagley.
"There it is!" she yelled.
"Honk honk," called the
dinosaur, softly.

The sound was so calming
that everyone stopped.
"Oh. My my," sighed Mrs.
Bagley. "How delightful."

Daisy hugged the Hadrosaur. "Don't lock him up," she begged.

"Of course not," replied Mrs. Bagley gently. "I have a much better idea."

The dinosaur was given a special home at the museum. And every day, people waited for hours to hear the Honking Hadrosaur's calming concerts.

Most of the dinosaur names in this book are the real ones used by dinosaur experts. Here's how to say them — the parts of the word in **bold** should be stressed.

	say...
Kritosaurus	Krit-oh-**saw**-rus
Megalosaurus	**Mega**-low-**saw**-rus
Raptor	**Rap**-tor
Ceratosaurus	Ser-at-oh-**saw**-rus
Spinosaurus	**Spine**-oh-**saw**-rus
Tarbosaurus	**Tar**-bo-**saw**-rus
Pliosaur	**Plee**-oh-**saw**
Allosaurus	**Al**-oh-**saw**-rus
Pteranodon	Ter-**an**-oh-don
Baryonyx	**Bar**-ee-**on**-iks
Cacops	**Ka**-kops
Saltopus	**Sal**-to-pus
Pterodactylus	**Ter**-oh-**dak**-til-us
Tyrannosaurus	Tie-**ran**-oh-**saw**-rus
Compsognathus	Komp-sog-**nath**-us
Stegoceras	Steg-**oss**-er-ass
Hadrosaur	**Had**-ro-**saw**

This edition first published in 2007 by Usborne Publishing Ltd.,
Usborne House, 83-85 Saffron Hill, London EC1N 8RT, England.
www.usborne.com
Copyright © 2007, 2006 Usborne Publishing Ltd.

48